Invasion Z:
The Final Battle for the Survival of the Planet

Aiden ziff

"The only easy day was yesterday." NAVY SEAL

Foreword

In the blink of an eye, Earth has been invaded by a hostile alien race with a diabolical plan. They have taken over six continents and annihilated the world's two superpowers: Russia and China. The world is on the brink of extinction.

The American continent is the only place that has avoided total destruction. For some unknown reason, it has not been attacked yet. But this temporary refuge could disappear at any moment.

The United States, along with its Latin American allies, have joined forces to confront the unknown threat that endangers the existence of humanity. The 6th team of the SEALs, considered the best special forces on the planet, are ready to take action. But even they wonder if it is possible to stop these alien invaders and save the world.

Index

1

Year 2030 - **World population**: 10 billion

Terror has come to our world. Half the planet has been invaded by a race from the stars. Many call them aliens, others call them extraterrestrials. The government simply calls them invaders. The planet has panicked, unprepared for such a thing... many fear the end.

A colossal mother ship has established a base on the African continent. The entire planet has been taken over. The only world powers that remained could not face it, only the American continent is free from the oppression of these beings of dark morphology, with fearsome appearance. Of a meter eighty of stature and strange elongated claws with oval heads and diabolical eyes like coal, they sow terror... their technology possibly according to the experts is around 200 years more advanced than the human one. We are lucky in theory, not to have been invaded by a race millions of years older.

The United States in the confrontation two weeks ago lost a million soldiers. They have the technology to defuse nuclear bombs so there is no choice. The only way to confront them is conventional warfare with firearms.

After the crash, the aliens have remained passive for several days outside the American continent. It is not known what they are up to... but neither is the only existing power wasting any time. The United States has been frantically gathering more volunteers to go again. Despite the conflicts between them before this, the governments of the continent have been secretly forming an alliance to make the penultimate defense of humanity. The Americans have assembled in record time of seven days; more than a million soldiers, and are heading for the African continent, where the dozens of alien ships that attacked the planet a few weeks ago have apparently been stopped. Russia has been defeated and 99% of its population has died, they could not contain the invasion. The Chinese government in four days was completely annihilated and 99% of its population, and so with the same method the other countries were wiped out by these creatures with slightly more advanced technology.

A few weeks ago the US forces waged war in the Persian Gulf, but they did not prevail, and about a million of their soldiers were annihilated. Now the last million remaining militias are going to face this threat. It is humanity's only hope. Mexico and all the Latin American countries, as well as Brazil, are gathering a colossal force known as the American alliance with more than four million soldiers, and they are marching alongside the U.S. forces in their warships and aircraft carriers. The world knows that if this last bastion fails to do battle; there will be nothing to stop them.

In the morning the President of the United States Samuel Blade gives a continental speech to give moral support to his armed forces and the nation. It is not known what the reason for this invasion is, except that they leave only 0.1% of people on each continent. They know very well that, if they do not contain them, the American continent and last bastion will be taken. The only ones that the Secretary of Defense left in the United States are the SEALS Group 6, the best on the planet for the care of the President and his family, in Mexico the F.E.R. and so on, the special forces of each country.

February 30. The American mainland force on its way to Africa is attacked by alien forces in the Baltic bar, most of the 5 million are wiped out, as well as all the submarines and ships. Only 50 helicopters and fighter planes manage to reach the Estonian-Russian border and land a few hundred tanks and infantry. In that battle, the American forces and a bastion of 5,000 Cuban and Venezuelan soldiers who accompanied them faced those creatures from the stars in the Estonian mountains... but they did not resist long, and were defeated in approximately four hours when the signal to the United States ceased. Few of the enemy have fallen in comparison to the humans, at this point there is no more hope it seems-.

The President of the United States gives a last message to humanity: "We have fallen, there is nothing to do but obey our instinct; flee or fight. Our forces have been beaten, the enemy is unknown and stronger than us. There is no escape, we have to fight. In this country there are 300 million souls, minimum every family has a rifle, fight for your children fight for your loved ones... I repeat, our armed forces have fallen in the Baltic Sea and a part in the mountains of Estonia, the signal has been cut, we do not know when the hostile forces will reach us, but we know it is imminent. America will always fight to the end...brothers of the earth, my brothers, fight."

Most of the earth is being consumed, fast ships of these beings already control almost the entire planet. The beings with frightening aspect and pronounced musculature come down from their ships to hunt the few survivors and take them to their ships... the mystery of why they leave 0.1 % of children of each continent is still unknown.

Special Forces Group 6 SEALS the best special forces force on the planet, take the president and his family, and some elite members to a secret base in Yellowstone. Some millionaires travel to their own emergency bunkers.

At this point money has ceased to be worth..., commercial stores are being looted, there is total chaos and anarchy in the streets. The law ceases to exist, people are hysterical for fear of dying, the police have disintegrated.

SEALS TEAM 6 is composed of 50 of the best on the planet. Its members are under the age of 31, and are experts in all kinds of combat, weapons handling, and even activating and deactivating nuclear weapons. Its commander is the military **Will Michael, the** best combat military in the history of the SEALS. He has participated in countless secret missions in Afghanistan, Iraq, Isis, among others, with a high success rate. Their mission now is to reach Antarctica as soon as possible and activate the negative energy neutrino-nuclear bomb that the United States had been secretly developing years before. And then, they must take a submarine and get to Africa to the alien mother ship that is somewhere in some Nigerian jungle.

2

Yellowstone Bunker

President Samuel Blade: boys, on your shoulders you have the future of humanity... the mission is clear, if you don't succeed there will be no choice but to take plan B. You are our last hope. I know of your ability and of all the history of this group; that has never failed, so we trust you.

Commander Will Michael: Mr. President, for us it is an honor to have served our country, our life ahead, for the nation is our motto, therefore, do not hesitate; we will fight to the end-.

The U.S. security group headed by Mike Gigald ordered only twenty-five SEALS and Will Michael to leave for Antarctica immediately. The other half of this group would stay behind and would be commanded by the decorated Major Arthur Glos and would leave immediately from Yellowstone. There they would meet up with all the special forces from some Latin American countries that sent their last force to support at that time, they were 1000 in total and would symbolically fight in the Pentagon City in Washington as a symbol of human power.

Hours later - Washington D.C.

Arthur Glos: Gentlemen, our colleagues have just left for the most important mission on earth; to reach Antarctica and go to Africa. We, along with the coalition of specials forcé from all over the Americas, will do battle here in Washington. You only have a few minutes to say goodbye to your families on the phone, and then we have to disperse... the invaders will surely arrive in a few hours, we know we won't win, but we want to take as many of those sons of bitches with us.

Thousands of people are fleeing to the mountains, lakes and seas. Panic begins to corrode the souls of most, many are killing themselves in hysterics over their impending destruction.

TEAM 6 of the SEALS marches at full speed in five military units to a complex two hours from Yellowstone hidden in the mountains, with the objective of taking a plane and fly immediately at speed to the subway base located in Antarctica, where is the last weapon of the USA, which in theory was unable to be detected by these creatures because it had innovative technology, but that was the first step .... the weak point was that by that time most of the satellites would be destroyed and would not work, so TEAM 6 would take a small satellite in the submarine to the jungle of Nigeria where the colossal mother ship was and try to get as close as possible and place the satellite in operation to teledirect the neutrino bomb of negative energy that is in Antarctica, and thus eliminate the standard of these creatures which is their origin ship.

3

A few kilometers from reaching the bunker the first team.
2:00 pm in the afternoon
Cloudy weather.

At this moment, the military convoy is speeding along a dirt road, immersed in rugged terrain. They are all dressed in black with their rifles and tactical vests. Some are chatting in the military unit where Major Will is riding.

Private Ben Aston: it's a suicide mission my friends, the kind we love..., at least I made love to my girl yesterday, I hope you did the same to your girlfriend Jorge, because you will never feel her warmth again...

Soldier Jorge Martinez: Aha. Don't say crazy things brother, you know we have nerves of steel, that's why we were created, but you know what? I didn't even have a chance, that's what makes me angry, but....

Now, boys, don't argue nonsense," said one of his companions who was in the copilot's seat. Corporal Anderson L.

-I wish I had a girl like you," said Private Rayan Black, who was sitting in the back seat and chewing his gum superbly, "I wish I had a girl like you.

Corporal Anderson: don't be slimy Rayan, I'll blow your brains out if you don't shut up, I'm not a bitch like the one who bore you....

Ryan Black: That's what they all say, but they eat it up.

-Your mother Rayan," joked Jorge Martinez.

Corporal Anderson: thank you Jorge for silencing the chicken Rayan, lately Rayan you have become an idiot.

Rayan Black: surely you liked me.

Corporal Anderson: I like you, ha! don't make me laugh.

Rayan Black: Well, since I am part of TEAM 6 you have a terrible temper. I can feel that I'm stirring up your hormones, we alphas always provoke that...

-End of discussion, guys," **ordered** Will, who was behind the wheel and accelerating the jeep at 180 km per hour through that lonely forest, hoping that those ships would not come out of the trees, otherwise it would be terrible.

Private Jack; Commander Will, we have arrived at the cave, all clear, but we have bad news. - Said a subordinate over the radio.

Will: what's up soldier? Speak...

Private Jack: Those things have just arrived in Brazil, and part of South America is already under attack... communication was lost a few minutes ago with our informant, but I'm afraid they are coming forward sir.

Will: Thank you, we'll be there in five minutes, get everything ready.

Rayan Black: bitch, we'll load the shit..., those things are coming.

Jorge Martínez: you can stop fucking around Rayan, can't you see that...

Rayan Black: Whatever the faggot says, you've become just like that bitch of a...

Will: We're finally here guys, do you copy? Sergeant Mark, Sanders, Peter, hurry up, we're here.

The SEALS team arrived at the bunker hidden in the Wyoming mountains. The small military plane was one of the few survivors of the colossal armament that the United States had before the invasion. In this ship it would take them at least a few hours to reach South Antarctica where the bunker, called the sugar cavern, was located.

Private Jack: commander, we are refueling, logistical problems, you know....

Will: Never mind soldier, let's go with the rest that are waiting for us. Now I want you to pay attention. -He said as he got out of the vehicle inside the bunker, and took a document out of a briefcase and proceeded to read it.

Antarctic bunker sugar cavern report

February 30, 2030, 3 pm.

Project X

Southeast location between the Ribeo and Montain skull mountains. Dimensions: 1000 M2.

Nuclear neutral test room for advanced weapons.

The mission is clear, all SEALS 6 team members are informed to wear safety gear to where the bomb is located. It does not emit radiation, but it does emit dark waves that disintegrate cells.

*The dark energy neutrino weapon is on the second floor of the nuclear neutrino test room. The access code is **123benjamintrimp.***

The destructive power of this neutral nuclear weapon has already been tested in a secret mission taken in 2023 to the planet Mars, specifically to one of its moons, and caused an explosion that crushed one eighteenth of its mass. The bomb in front of you is much less powerful, but capable of eliminating a range of 50 km around it. Be warned that this mission is 99% certain to kill you once the device reaches Nigeria. The pencil bomb will traverse at breathtaking speed across the sea until it reaches the Nigerian jungle where you will redirect it with the small satellite, and then it will explode with the active dark neutrino element. There will be no time to escape. To activate it, you will only be required to enter the code **AWSFJUE867usa** and the time from its start of activation to its location in Nigeria will be 80 hours.

His president and friend Samuel Blade, and the safety board to safeguard human life-.

WILL: You heard the main thing guys, the rest is protocol. It sounds pretty sad, but it's our job. Most likely none of us will come back, but remember, we will do it for our families or for anyone who survives from this world once we blow the main stronghold of those beasts to pieces. Remember, our families are in the bunker so we fight fiercely," said Commander Will, barely revealing a smile of pride and bravery.

4

-We are with you, commander," they all shouted.

Private Jack: Commander, the aircraft is ready.

-Let's go then," Will ordered.

The turtle-shaped, lead-colored alien ships are ravaging Colombia, Venezuela and some Caribbean islands with voracity. Thousands are being taken in other ships with elongated tubes sucking them from the ground, specifically young specimens. Know for what purpose. The fact is that no one so far has a theory in the scientific community.

3 p.m.: the T45IH aircraft flies at full speed towards the southeast region of Antarctica, as marked by the GPS of a satellite that is still working. Everyone is silent except Rayan and 3 or 4 others arguing as usual.

Private Ben: Commander, do you have any idea what the hell those things are looking for out there?

The commander was looking ahead, but responded with -I don't know, but it's not good what's coming, I don't like the fact that they only leave 0.1% survivors.

-Maybe a human farm... I've heard that on the mystery channels like; Spanish Vmgramisterio or nonsense like that -Said Rayan mocking Jorge for being of Spanish descent.

-That may be," argued Private Ben.

Private Mark: I don't know, but those things are not pretty, did you see them boss?

Will nodded without looking at Mark's face.

One of the fiercest soldiers in combat and a veteran of TEAM 6 who almost never said anything, spoke up.

Feder Raser: the idea is not far-fetched, most likely we will serve as food for those races, but in the future.

- What are you talking about Raser? -said Ben.

-If you have noticed, none of the few videos that have been captured show them devouring humans. And the logical thing for an alien race is to study us, you know, the issue of pathogens, viruses, can be counterproductive even for them who are not so technologically advanced to us. I say this because of their ships that still use some kind of fuel for the beam they leave, even if they are not sonorous..., and they know well what it means to use fuel... they are surely from a nearby solar system, not far away.

-Applause for the brain," Ryan said loudly.

Will: it has logic... - Said the commander somewhat thoughtfully.

Corporal Anderson: Good theory Felder. viruses! in fact, I'm sure it's something they're afraid of. It must be a species that goes around the stars consuming races, and when they arrive to this world full of life they want to leave us as a farm, a lot of meat. But the predictable thing is that if your theory is true; first they will study us, previously they must have experienced epidemics, that's why they don't want to take any risks.

- Since when are you guys scientists here? -muttered Rayan sitting at the end of where everyone was sitting.

Some made faces, others ignored it.

Arthur Glos: SEALS team copy me.

Will: we copy you loud and clear my friend, any news?

Arthur Glos: they have not arrived here yet, but most of the radio antennas have been destroyed, there are only a few left, and as you know, they are in Mexico..., and they are annihilating everything.

-All right commander, let's just hope we get our butts on the ice soon and get this over with....

Arthur Glos: I hope there is no news, and everything goes according to plan.

Will: we hope so, how long do you expect these things to arrive?

Arthur Glos; I don't know, but a group of black ships already entered, unknown until now, accompanying the metallic ones, and they are killing everything southwest of Mexico, maybe tomorrow morning they will be arriving here, they are not using bombs, they are using something worse commander.

Will: what are you using?

Arthur Glos: I'm not sure, but they are like ALIENS, that's not what our contact said.

Will: Aliens? what are you talking about, if they are the ALIENS.

Arthur Glos: I know boss, but these things are horrifying. According to the pictures and videos they sent a few hours ago, you can see how fast they are, added to their diabolical morphology with pointed teeth and black flesh, they move like small rapacious dinosaurs, with the difference that these are swarms, and they are using them by the tens of thousands; destroying everything in their path.

Will: thanks for the tip, we will be in touch if those things allow it, Commander Arthur.

-Copied.

5

Most of the American continent has been devastated, hundreds of millions have died in just about 8 hours, there are no defenses left, only lower California and part of Chihuahua remain intact, but it is only a matter of time before the swarm of ships arrives, and release the swarms of beasts of the universe and devour the entire population of those places, perhaps at night.

The SEAL team has already arrived in Antarctica, and have parachuted into inaccessible terrain leaving the old aircraft in the air without a pilot, only to fall into a lake and plunge into the depths minutes later. They are heading towards the sugar cave, it's a few hours of dangerous landscape and full of gorges, that one false step could be a deadly fall.

Commander Arthur and the coalition of Latin American special forces as a whole 1000 soldiers are already deployed in several strategic locations in Washington. It will be the last battle.

Private Steve: Commander Arthur, do you think they will make it?

- What are those questions soldier? How many times has SEAL Team 6 failed? Never. It's unforgivable to fail, and even if those things are otherworldly, they won't go clean. -refuted the commander.

Private Kelsy: more faith, boy... you're in the Seals for nothing, did you forget when we were sent to rescue Senator A.D. in the Russian prison full of Spetsnaz who were said to be the best? well only 15 of us went in there and wiped them all out, and we left clean... that proves that TEAM 6 is a different level.

-I understand. -said the young soldier Steve.

Arthur Glos: Soldiers stand by, communications have already been cut off on the Mexican side, San Diego California will most likely be attacked tonight. Unfortunately millions will die, there is nothing we can do but wait for those sons of bitches to show up and unload our .50 calibers.

With a long, "Yes," they shouted in jubilation TEAM 6 number 2 as they dispersed to their posts and Private Kelsy and the commander stayed behind chatting. While some of the Latin American special forces in the distance could be heard cheering each other on, speaking in their own languages.

Private Kelsy: Commander Arthur, at least you have a wife and two children that you will leave if this does not...

Arthur Glos: Kelsy..., you...

-Commander, it's not every day you meet love and you say yes, let's have children. I always loved this war thing, but this is different...I'm going childless, something I was looking forward to having in about 10 when I was 35, you know, already having a heritage and having been part of this team.

-Girl, I'm 35 and I see you as my daughter, come on give me a hug! You'll get out of this and I'll come to your wedding.

-We know, commander, that there will be no turning back.

-Come, let me hug you," he said as he held her tightly and calmed her down. -I promise you they will not leave intact, believe me, they have never faced the most efficient elite force on the planet.

In Antarctica, team 6 has arrived a little late, but safely at the gates of the bunker that is camouflaged as a natural part of the snow on the mountain. The landscape is inhospitable, it's freezing cold, but at least they are lucky for now that these things are not yet flying in the skies.

Corporal Anderson: Do you know if there are any scientists still working in there, sir?

Will: they've been empty for a couple of weeks...

Jorge Martinez: Let's open this gate, I despair to see this landscape without any tree. It's depressing, I feel we are being spied on from afar. Hurry up Rayan! I see you have already lost some talent in hacking this access.

Rayan: wait, don't be an ass, don't you see it's encrypted..., it's opening. I hope a little ALIENS doesn't come out as a welcome because I'll blow his brains out.

Will: you can shut the fuck up, Rayan," commanded the commander, - order that the soldier respectfully obeyed-.

-Listen, no games inside, understood?

-Understood, sir. -They all replied.

Will: we will split up, Anderson and company come with me, Rayan, Jorge John and 5 more, go and look for the small submarine where we will go to Nigeria, hurry up, let's go! -Rayan: don't forget to close the entrance.

It took them about twenty-five minutes to reach the second floor of the bunker. At the bottom of some metal stairs was the section where the dark neutri-nuclear bomb was located. On the other side the second group found a small submarine ready to leave, it was a new prototype, but faster than most and theoretically undetectable.

Corporal Anderson; what the hell! commander What is this thing?

Will: it doesn't look like a bomb, it looks like something out of this world, right down to its design.

Felder: as far as we know there has never been extraterrestrial contact, otherwise they wouldn't have said so. Most of the speculation then was about the technology of the powers of those years, wow, but this thing is strange, a form of... in the shape of a pencil with pulsating lights around it.

Will: the report did not say anything about its manufacture nor did it allude to images. What it does say is that it is very rare.

Weterson: It looks like something out of a movie, Commander.

Will: well team, we don't have time for assumptions, I'll believe this thing was built by america. It seems like a strange technology to me, but we're here to activate it not create theories. I still don't know how this thing will fly, it doesn't make sense a bomb shaped like a pencil and a star on the tip, but hey, we're not engineers.

Felder: I agree...

Will: copy me Rayan, tell me the activation key.

Rayan: copied. **AWSFJUE867usa.**

Jorge copies me, have you located the submarine yet?

Jorge Martinez: affirmative sir, we are just waiting for them....

Will: copied, now let's go....

Anderson: You heard it guys, get your asses moving, 500 meters up is the submarine, move it.

The city of Washington looks empty and without chaos in the streets unlike some cities on the west coast. Where 50% of its population has fled to the forests or other counties. Only 50% stayed in their homes. There are armed men remaining throughout the city, they will wage war according to their actions. The special forces of the SEALS and company are in the center of the capital, they have all kinds of anti-armor weapons, mortars and rocket launchers, they will give everything when they see those things coming.

Somewhere in Washington

Sergeant Angela: Sir, what are you thinking, why are you alone here?

Arthur Glos: nothing, just waiting for a radio signal, but nothing. Most likely they are now attacking San Diego or Los Angeles. On the radio they warned that ships were approaching, but something destroyed the radio antennas and I didn't hear anything more.

Sergeant Angela: I never see fear in your eyes commander, I would like to be like you.

Arthur Glos: remember, we all feel fear, but everyone shows it in different ways. Fear is necessary, don't forget it. You look tired, go on, get some sleep, it's a little late.

Sergeant Angela: I'll take your word for it sir, I'll need energy, you rest too.

Arthur Glos: Then go.

6

Antarctic bunker 10 p.m. Atlantic Sea offshore Nigeria

Rayan Black: Damn! I'm so fucked up, and to think that this summer I was going to visit some brothels in Japan...

Private Mike Brown: you never change bro, and do you like Japanese girls or why do you go there? Are there no good asses here in America or is it a morbid fetish?

Rayan Black: I have a fixation for skin color and their private things, they drive me crazy. Besides, according to me, there is less gonorrhea over there, - he said leering at Corporal Anderson who was sitting in front of him, and she looked annoyed and responded furiously.

Corporal Anderson: take your damn eyes off my sick..., boss, I'll break your...

Will: Stop it, you look like little kids. Can't you see we're going on the most important mission in history and you're like cats and dogs fighting. If you have something, come on! come on! fistfight now and end your constant bickering...

Corporal Anderson: no problem for me, let's do it," said the woman, taking off her tactical vest and leaving her M4 carbine rifle on her seat.

Rayan was silent, but Will gave him the order to accept.

Will: Come on Rayan! the way you talk, show him what you're made of. Give me two minutes of all-out combat, put down your weapons and show what you're capable of, and stop this bullshit about throwing shit at each other.

Two minutes later Rayan, one of the best snipers in the world and a very capable military man, was lying on the floor humiliated by a beautiful 24 year old woman, one of the best in SEAL Team 6. On the sides of the submarine sat the rest of the team watching in astonishment.

Jorge Martinez: Come on, shake hands Rayan, I expect you to behave yourself after a lady has played your ass.

Fuck you, Jorge, I'm going to shove my gun up your ass. - he said and went out to another furious behavior with some bruises on his cheekbones, but nothing serious for such a tough guy.

- Commander, we are approaching the coast of Nigeria," warned Private Peter, who was driving the submarine at full power, from the cockpit.

Washington D.C., 1 p.m. The 1,000 or so special forces accompanying the SEALS take turns keeping watch at night. There's Mexico's F.E.R., Guatemala's KAIBILES, Colombia's AFEUR, Brazil's BOPE, among many others.

The alien force of hundreds of fast-moving ships is already flying through the skies of Texas and Oklahoma, and they are about to arrive. A gigantic swarm follows the ships closely; it is a plague of voracious beasts, something unusual and they eat everything. Their fangs and snouts are horrifying, it takes at least two 50 caliber bullets to stop one of these things that weigh about 150 kilos to 200 kilos, and possess a triple skin similar to that of a crocodile, but with a different texture and color. The ALIENS minds that control the ships no longer come down, only from above they launch spheres filled with a kind of lava-like shrapnel that sinks into people's flesh killing them in the worst way. They also release a type of toxin that begins to paralyze humans and they are easy prey for these creatures named **Styles**. No one would have believed that the world would come to this. It was estimated that a total of about 5 thousand millionaires and top government officials have taken refuge in their bunkers around the planet to survive this apocalypse.

Yellowstone Bunker Safety Table. 6 A.M. March 2.

Counselor Albert R: Mr. President, the last message has arrived. After this there will be no more; everything has collapsed, they are about to reach the last bastion of special forces in Washington D.C. We don't know when they won't find us here in California. By now those outer ships must be up there looking for all traces of intelligent life to eliminate it.

President Samuel Blade: I understand. I still remember when NASA warned of a colossal strange swarm heading for earth on January 12, 2030, and everyone thought it was simple asteroids...I asked the senate to send a probe to rule out anything intelligent that might be dangerous, but I only received 5 votes and was not allowed to send anything.

Councilor Albert: I know, it was a brutal mistake on their part. Two weeks ago we realized it was something we never anticipated: intelligent life, and they were coming towards us, but it was too late to launch any attack.

Councilor McMillan: They arrived on February 15, just deep in the Nigerian forest. We quickly sent state-of-the-art fighters to reconnoiter and they never came back...that's when we realized by Mayday that they were hostile.

President Samuel Blade: I think we will only live on memories if SEALS TEAM 6 does not succeed in the mission. By now, if everything went well, they have probably arrived.

Chief Counselor Lucas: I agree with you, Chairman.

Councilor Albert: it is a very powerful race sir, the government of Nigeria in 6 hours was wiped out as well as its population, and that is when the major potentials became alarmed. Russia attempted a full scale nuclear attack, and that's when we all went into dread; those things were capable of defusing nuclear attacks with unknown technology. So Russia launched the most powerful military attack ever launched, and they did it hand in hand with China, but unfortunately some 5,000 alien ships tore them to pieces in the Indian Sea heading for Africa.

The United States, seeing that in 5 days the entire forces of the world powers were wiped out, we tried to make peace, but these creatures did not even try; they attacked us. That is when we launched the first operation of 1 million 300 thousand soldiers, but our men were exterminated in the Baltic Sea, that is when we decided to launch the last one and the rest is history.

President Samuel Blade. What I wondered and apparently we will never know, why did these things come to our world? could it be true what the conspiracy theorists said? they come to colonize us, that's why apparently in some areas they are leaving remains of children, but why? the second thing of annihilating the majority is pure sadism, of that I am sure.

Chief Advisor Lucas: it is strange their behavior, maybe we will never find out we can only deduce, but the fact is that they have now eliminated 90% of humanity, and now they are heading to the remaining part of our nation; to finish their job-.

At one point in the conversation among some elite members of what was once the most powerful nation in the world, something unexpected happened.

President Samuel Blade: He resigned," said the president with a determined voice.

- What did you say, sir? - all the advisors asked in chorus.

-I said I quit, there is no reason to be president anymore, he quit. Even if the mission of our guys was successful, the world will not need presidents, they will only need to survive. How many years is there food in here? 5 or 10 years, I appreciate everyone's life, I do not want to be locked up here, it is better to give my place to all the SEALS family who are here. In this small place of no more than 2,000 m2.

Samuel Blade: as last minute president ordered the 200 of the secret service that are still with me to accompany me, you will remain in command and do the prudent thing, my friend.

After those words Mr. President Samuel Blade and a group of 200 secret service armed with m16 rifles went out somewhere in Yellowstone to confront the ALIENS, but to their surprise they found nothing, only destruction and chaos. There were only charred, mangled corpses and fresh skeletons and a few downed ships, but there was no sign of the alien offensive still around.

7

Washington D.C. 10 a.m. before the battle, formation of the SEALS and the rest of the Latin American special forces.

Will: formation. They're coming up, everyone to your posts, they'll be here in a few minutes. - he shouted. Will: -No need to be afraid boys. Fight as if you were children, don't be afraid, heaven awaits us..., you know, not only alien ships are coming destroying everything in their path, underneath those ships they release thousands and thousands of little devouring beasts, so there will be fun boys. Half to the buildings, the other half with me, prepare the rocket launchers and the small missiles, you are going to taste a little of the power... you Latin American special forces, thank you! let's give them a little of the human fury. -he said in a loud voice.

After the words of the commander Arthur Glos, the team was divided one at the top of a building, and with Arthur; Steve, Kelsy, Angela among others down in the military cars. In the same direction in other avenues were already formed the special forces of all Latin American countries. At this hour they have already eliminated all the people in all the counties and the smaller dark ships are heading towards Washington and are counted by hundreds. The lead-colored, tortoise-shell-shaped ships are the ones destroying crops and forests with fire, and from them these beasts descend in millions, devouring entire cities in hours.

On the African continent, TEAM 6 has already landed in the Gulf of Guinea. And they are already immersed in the mountains of Cameroon... it will take them a few hours to get deep into the Nigerian jungle without being seen. Everything looks desolate, hundreds and hundreds of Cameroonian towns ravaged by the beasts or whatever kind of creatures from the stars that have brought those aliens that are already taking to the skies of most of the planet. China the colossus from space looks funereal, its 2 billion people who once inhabited it have perished. Proud and impregnable Russia with all its nuclear arsenal has been wiped off the face of the earth, as have most of the powerful countries and their entire population. So far on the morning of March 2nd at least 9.5 billion people have been annihilated in an apocalyptic Armageddon, and now it is minutes away from reaching the only point on earth that the destructive machinery has not yet reached; Washington D.C. Plus about 3 nearby states that have panicked and started to flee to the forests to Seattle to the icy areas of Canada, but in vain... these creatures that devour everything on the ground and the ships in the air give no truce, it will be useless; Canada is being devoured right now; Quebec is resisting, but not for long, they are millions of wild beasts released from those ships to hunt their prey; the humans.

SEALS and Special Forces are ready to give the last of human strength in the last symbolic battle for humanity, Some of the SEALS sing the song "we are the champions" by Queen. The Mexican F.ERs sing "cielito lindo", and so they rejoice in their last minutes of life as they go into action against the alien invasion. Their families, their loved ones are the last memories they will have. There is not much to think about when you are about to enter the line of death.

12 o'clock. Dark ships are making their way through Washington, there are thousands of men shooting all over the city at things moving too fast over the ground and through the air. The 50 calibers shake the streets with their power and the devouring fire of the ALIENS ships fall from the sky lighting up entire streets. They give no respite, they are efficient and voracious... the experience in destroying life on the worlds is clearly seen. Minutes later the gray ships enter and from the sky they drop things like giant eggs and from them come out thousands and thousands of creatures bigger than a tiger, but much faster and more terrifying with dark skin and strange red green eyes, that devour the whole brain, not even a .223 caliber burst stops one, you need a .50 caliber straight to the head. Little by little they are devouring, destroying everything, with the help of the ships above that launch electric rays and shrapnel-like guts. The objective is clearly to eliminate everything, here they are apparently leaving nothing alive... their attack is ferocious, they are swarms of different kinds of things that move very fast. They are clearly ferocious creatures captured from distant galaxies possibly by these beings to devastate worlds for their bestiality-.

Johnny: that song is good Jorge, we are the champions we are the la la la la la la la la la, although to tell the truth I prefer to die fighting with the Queen song, that Bohemian Rhapsody song is a gem.

Soldier Steve: my mom used to sing that song to me as a kid that's why I love rock and hate Regueton shit.

Kelsy: they are coming guys....

Arthur Glos: Guys, let's show these things that they'll hit a wall, I think it's a nice day for...

Kelsy: no commander, don't say it... Comrades it was a pleasure to have had so many experiences and missions together. Thank you all. It will be nice to fight to the end with comrades..., and you Angela, I know it wasn't much to your liking, come on! give me a hand! don't be a pussy, - said Kelsy making the proud Angela shake her hand.

F.E.R. soldiers: here they come. -They shouted loudly from the side of a street.

March 2, 2030. The invasion machine has reached the center of Washington. It has razed everything in its path, nothing has stopped it, the beasts do not seem to back down for anything, although there are alien ships that have fallen, the damage they have received is minimal, some say they were 10 shot down, but it is nothing for the hundreds that are nearby advancing. The special forces group of 1000 has held out longer than everyone so far, putting up a fight and impeding at times the advance of the beasts and ships, and taking down about 5 ships in one attack thanks to the powerful missile fire that the SEALS and Argentine special forces have been firing and have proven their mettle in combat. Peruvian special forces have impressed in ground combat with these creatures giving the defense some breathing room at times.

Arthur Glos: fire, do not cease, (shouts) -Johnny fires the missile at the ships above, at the approaching ones hurry up!

It was about 6 intense hours under hostile attack, unfortunately all were eliminated except 5 members of TEAM six who lie in the dark under the rubble of collapsed buildings. Some beasts left behind are still devouring corpses that are still badly wounded.

Corporal Anderson: Commander, are you all right?

Arthur Glos: fuck. I thought I was dead and had arrived in hell in total darkness. Oh damn! Did you see? We put up a fight, but those damn ships... Is that you Johnny?

Johnny: yes sir, I think I fucked up my elbow, I'm apparently lower than you guys.

Arthur Glos: stay there, we'll try to get out.

Angela: here we are also commander, me and Steve, unfortunately I think everyone else died, when that ship threw that thing into the building and collapsed it.

Arthur Glos: I'm glad boys, we just have to try to get out of here, although out there you can still hear those damn monsters and they are surely sniffing the corpses below, they want to eat us for sure. Our only advantage is that the ships are moving forward... unfortunately in the next 15 hours it will all be over; about 90 million will die and they are the last ones on earth.

Kelsy: Don't worry, Commander.

Arthur Glos: Johnny I'll throw the flashlight at you.

Johnny: Thank you, it will be a great help.

Eight hours later, with great effort and exhausting maneuvers, they managed to get out of the rubble of the building that had been previously demolished, and thanks to the fact that it fell on top of another building, they did not die.

Private Steve: Shit, they destroyed everything boss.

Arthur Glos: no time for sentimentality. Ready with your weapons there may be more of those things out there. I see that no one was left alive of our comrades, even the bones were eaten. - said the commander looking around him.

Kelsy: what shall we do now, sir? they have eliminated everything," said the girl looking around with her mouth open.

Arthur Glos: First time I don't know what to answer, but at least we are alive. For now let's go up to one of those buildings that are still standing. There is evidence that they eliminated everything there, but... come on! move! later we will think about what to do... for now we will have to survive tonight.

Angela: the boss is right, I think it's profitable to be alive for now, let's move better.

Private Steve: I'll take these weapons and magazines with me," said the soldier as he picked up some ak-47 rifles on the ground and quickly threw them into a bag.

Unfortunately, this diabolical race did not like the fact that they had enough ship casualties, so hours later they launched a boson bomb so powerful that it eliminated all of Washington from the face of the earth, thus destroying the only survivors of TEAM 6 in that place.

8

Deep in the Nigerian jungle

1 a.m.

The TEAM 6 command has arrived safely with the small satellite in sight. The only thing left to do is to reach the huge spacecraft, probably about 30 km inland. They are tired, so they will sleep that night there, in the undergrowth. The mission has gone perfectly, they have not yet encountered those beasts, something strange for no one to guard the mother ship at that distance, they have only seen those ships at speed that are lost out of sight on the horizon. Mind you, tomorrow it will surely be all over if they make it past those maybe 30 km that separates them from their target. Everything will explode at a range of 50 km so they will most likely all die. From Antarctica to Nigeria the bomb will do a maximum of 10 minutes, so they will not have time to escape.

March 3 9 a.m.

Will: well, we only have the last 5 km left guys, the order is to get us as close as 500 meters, well we knew that we were all going to die by accepting such a mission, but, no. You guys go, I'll just go, come on! please turn around and run away... the mission is almost complete.

Of course not, Commander, we will be with you until death. -they all said.

Will: Come on Anderson, you're a young girl, you have a lot of life left to live.

Anderson, See you at the end, Will.

Rayan: With you until the end, sir.

Jorge: Same here

Felder: Me too.

The rest of the SEALS shouted, "With you, sir.

Will: if that's what they decided, I respect their decision, then let's move forward-.

At 11 a.m. They arrived 500 meters away from the colossal alien craft that was suspended over hundreds of trees a mere 10 meters above the ground. It was as big as a village, perhaps it could carry dozens of aircraft carriers inside. Hundreds of these ships were coming in and out of it... at the gates, one could see these thin creatures of diabolical aspect, but surely with intellect superior to humans, but also very cruel and hostile in their actions. Human beings were also perceived being transported in transparent capsules connected with something that resembled some kind of pulsating flesh tubes. At least 100 of them passed this way. There was no surveillance in theory, no creatures around. There were only glimpses of the impressive engineering etched into the material of that black mothership.

Will: guys we did it, I just activated the triangulation, the bomb will arrive in 10 minutes and counting. If what we were told is true; nothing will survive within 50 km, the explosion will be so powerful that it will cause tsunamis, even running won't be good, we could never run 50 km in 10 minutes -.

Some sat on some rocks resigned to die in a few minutes, Will went out into the open Anderson followed him out of the rest.

Anderson: now, for the first time I looked you in the eyes and I want to tell you thank you for being my platonic love all this time, don't say anything sir, just thank you. -Anderson confessed a little shyly. He swallowed saliva and said nothing, then without speaking to each other they both turned around and returned to the group.

Felder: If we are going to die here, why not commander...?

Will: what do you say gentlemen, you want to have fun for the last ten minutes before this shit flies.

TEAM SEAL: Let's dance jazz - they all shouted.

The 50-member special forces team deployed around the colossal ship, they knew they would not achieve anything they were even determined to make a frontal confrontation resigned to die, knowing that they would not lose anything because at that moment a bomb in the form of a neutri-nuclear pencil of dark energy was heading at an incredible speed with a colossal power thousands of times more powerful than the czar's bomb. They got wind of it and sent fighter ships. It was a frantic few minutes in the jungle... little by little they were falling..., the SEALS one by one gave their lives for the planet, but not before having eliminated more than 12 enemy ships.

Will and Anderson were fleeing without weapons even knowing that there was no escape, but the instinct of survival made them run and not give up. Seconds later a ship that was chasing them lost the route and crashed into the trees, from that small dark colored ship came out 3 diabolical beings with a fearsome aspect. Anderson and Will lay behind some bushes while those things looked at the ship and tried to fix it. It was 3 minutes before the explosion and Will thought of something.

Anderson: sir, look...

Will: There's almost nothing left, we'll explode here, there's no point in hiding, give me the gun.

Anderson: but what will you do?

Will: I don't care if we try anything, soon that thing will fall from the sky and.... you know I have an idea.

Anderson: What are you talking about?

Will: I'll blow the brains out of those things and we'll get out of here in that ship, see? they've already turned it back on and that's just what I wanted.

Anderson: but no...

Will: it doesn't matter if you die in an explosion or in an uncontrolled ship, honey.

Anderson: Did you say honey? -.

9

Seconds later Will fired the 15 projectiles at the heads of those humanoid shaped things, but anthropomorphic, something strange. They fell, although they were still moving, maybe they would not die because their skulls could regenerate themselves, it was something impressive. Quickly boarding the ship, both desperate humans with only two minutes of time crushed commands that looked strange trying to turn it on, until Will touched one on the top like a gear, and the ship began to rise to an uncertain direction, but at an amazing speed.

Within ten minutes the neutri-nuclear bomb exploded just as they had said, causing an apocalyptic explosion and pulverizing a radius greater than the predicted 100 km, causing a mega tsunami that wiped Nigeria off the map and most of the countries of the continent were under water.

Will and Anderson landed somewhere in the Amazon jungle, safe and sound. The invading race after seeing their mothership destroyed gradually left the planet for fear of something more powerful than them. Without a mothership they feared and left, saved the savage beasts of the stars without reasoning were still on the earth's soil, but it would be easier for the human race to emerge little by little. Will and Anderson had twin girls and as best they could they survived on amazon. Although 99.9% of the race was eliminated, it is expected that there are still about 3 million inhabitants scattered all over the planet, as there is still a fierce struggle for survival with those beasts from the stars that roam in large herds eating all forms of terrestrial life. But the planet is saved for now thanks to a group of soldiers who risked their lives; the TEAM 6 special forces of the United States.

Translated and Written by Commander: Will Michael.

End

Bonus content

The arrival of the strangers

Chapter 1: The arrival of the cursed beings

The night sky was clear and the stars were shining brightly. It was a quiet night in the world until something strange happened. A meteor shower lit up the sky and struck the Earth, causing a powerful earthquake on Earth. People got scared and ran in all directions to protect themselves.

But no one knew that these meteors were anything but ordinary. And it is that, there was a spaceship with evil aliens on board. An entity unknown to humanity was trying to conquer Earth and force humanity to follow its will and worship it.

Russia was the first country to notice the arrival of the cursed beings. His special forces, known as Cobra Commandos, were ready to deal with the threat. The US Special Forces team leader, Major General John Riker, received the news and joined the Russian effort to counter the invasion, despite having been enemy nations in the past.

Alien ships had landed in different parts of the world, from which cursed beings had emerged, with an infamous morphology and appearance. They were terrifying in appearance, with black, scaly skin and razor-sharp teeth. Within hours, their presence began wreaking havoc and destruction in cities around the world.

The national armies fought valiantly against the cursed beings, but were soon overwhelmed by the aliens' technological superiority. Only Russian and American special forces appear to have been able to hold the line.

And it is then, that General Riker and his team of the US Special Forces are sent to an American city invaded by cursed beings. The city was in ruins and people were fleeing in all directions. Buildings were on fire and aliens were everywhere.

Russian Cobra Special Forces joined General Riker's team as they marched through the city streets, fighting cursed beings around every corner. The battle seemed to go on forever, but the Special Forces were determined to fight to the end and save humanity from the alien invasion.

An invasion of cursed beings has begun and the fate of humanity hangs in the balance. Will the United States and Russia be able to save humanity?

Chapter 2: The Special Forces Alliance

Team Cobra and General Liker's team continued to advance through the city, fighting the cursed creatures throughout. As they progressed, they discovered that the aliens were not only strong and fast, but also highly intelligent. They used battle tactics that would surprise human soldiers and displayed superior technological prowess.

However, the special forces group did not give up. They stood together, fought bravely and skillfully, and managed to clear a part of the city. So, it was that at that moment, General Liker received a distress call from the head of the Japanese special forces. He informs her that the city of Tokyo is also under attack by cursed creatures and they need immediate help.

General Liker knew that he could not abandon the Japanese allies in their fight. So he gathered his team and the commander of the Russian Cobra, and together they boarded a military transport plane bound for Tokyo. During the flight, they discussed the situation and decided to form an alliance to face the cursed creatures.

When they landed in Tokyo, they found the city in ruins. Buildings were in ruins, streets were littered with rubble, and citizens were fleeing in all directions. The cursed creatures were wreaking havoc everywhere.

The special forces team launched their attack, marching through the streets of Tokyo and fighting against the cursed creatures. The Russian Cobra Commando also entered the fray, and together they formed a powerful force that was steadily advancing.

Then the special forces team discovered something strange. The cursed creatures seemed to be connected to some kind of technology, sharing information and abilities. It was as if they were working as a team, coordinating their attacks on a global scale.

General Liker and the Cobra leader realized they had to find a way to break the bond between the cursed creatures in order to have any chance of defeating them. Together they developed a device that hacked into alien technology and planted it in military units around the world.

An alliance of Russian, American and Japanese special forces worked tirelessly to defeat the cursed creatures. Eventually, they were able to cut the connection between the aliens, and the cursed beings lost their strength and coordination . The special forces then launched a final assault and succeeded in driving the cursed creatures from the earth.

Chapter 3: The truth about the invasion

As Russian, American, and Japanese special forces rid the city of the remnants of the alien invasion, General Liker began to ask questions. He wanted to know who were these cursed creatures and why had they invaded the earth?

After several weeks of investigation, General Liker learned the truth about the invasion. The cursed creatures were an alien race that had stalked humanity for decades. They saw humanity advancing technologically and decided to conquer the land and claim it as their own.

General Liker gathered the leaders of the Russian, American and Japanese special forces and explained the situation to them. Everyone was shocked by this news, realizing that humanity is constantly in danger of being attacked by advanced and malicious aliens.

Therefore, General Liker and the leaders of the Special Forces created a Global Defense Council dedicated to protecting Earth from future alien threats. The council worked in secret, gathering information and developing new technologies to protect humanity from potential invaders.

Chapter 4: The return of the cursed creatures

Months later...

Despite the efforts of the Global Defense Council, the cursed creatures have returned to Earth. They learned from their mistakes in the first invasion and developed new tactics and technologies to win this time.

General Liker and the leaders of the special forces responded quickly to the threat and gathered forces from all over the world to fight against the cursed creatures. This time the battle was even more fierce than before, and the cursed beings displayed superior skills and advanced tactics.

However, SWAT teams learned from their first victory against the cursed creatures and were better prepared this time. Using new technologies and tactics to fight the aliens, they managed to break their technological link again.

After several weeks of fierce fighting, the special forces finally managed to defeat the cursed creatures and save the earth once again. But this time they knew better than to lose their guard. They must continue to work together to protect humanity from future alien threats.

General Liker and the leaders of the Special Forces continued to work together in a Global Defense Council dedicated to protecting Earth from future threats. Mankind survived two alien invasions, but knew they had to be alert and ready for any potential threat.

Chapter 5: The Final Battle

Several years have passed since the last alien invasion. Humanity continues to work hard at the Global Defense Council to develop new technologies and strategies to protect itself from any potential threat. One day, the special forces saw a large group of spacecraft approaching Earth. They know it's an alien invasion, but this time it's different. The fleet was much larger than the previous ones, and the Special Forces unit knew that it would be the most important battle of their lives.

General Likker and the head of the Russian special forces gathered forces from all over the world to fight the aliens. This time they fight not only for the planet, but for all of humanity. They know that if they lose this battle, humanity is doomed.

The battle was fierce and the special forces fought fiercely with the aliens. The aliens have developed new technologies and advanced tactics, and the battle seems lost. However, the special forces did not give up. They fought with all their might knowing that they were fighting for humanity. Eventually, after many days of fierce fighting, the Special Forces successfully broke the technological link between the aliens and began defeating them one by one. The aliens realized that they had underestimated humanity's resolve and evacuated Earth. And even more, the army brought a new weapon that made the aliens vulnerable, it was a song at full volume, called: who poompo who pompo, who pompo, the marbles who pompo".

Humanity has overcome its greatest challenge yet, and General Leek and the leaders of the special forces realize that they have accomplished an incredible feat. They united the world in a common fight and showed that humanity is stronger when we work together. After the battle, General Likerr and the leaders of the Special Forces formed a new Global Defense Council tasked with protecting humanity from any potential threat. They know that there will always be danger in the universe, but they also know that as long as humans continue to cooperate, they can face anything. And so humanity moves on, knowing that they are more connected and stronger than ever.

The lkurus warrior
On a distant planet lived Lkurus,
A fearless and brave warrior. He held the sword strong to
protect the family,
A demon that fell from the sky, from another dimension.
They are trying to fulfill their mission. Lkurus knew that his
people were in danger,
The battle begins. His eyes flashed with great anger,
His sword glows with raw power. The enemy approached, but
he was not afraid,
With his skill and strength he did it. Demons howl when
wounded,
But hunger did not stop them. Lkurus fought hard,
Protect your family and your planet. The fight was hard, but he
did not waver,
Until the monsters are destroyed one by one. The sky clears, the
threat ends,
Lkurus felt triumphant, but also sad. The fighting was fierce and
the losses enormous.
Although his family was unharmed, grief overwhelmed him.
Lcurus knew that he would have to move on,
Because new threats may continue.

Despite the victory, Lkurus knew it wasn't over yet,
As they can come from other rooms,
Your skills need to be improved,
If you want your people to be protected.
Then he went to the top of the hill,
There a wise old man was waiting for him,

With the knowledge of the galaxy,
And the power that wisdom gave him. Lkurus listened attentively,
Courage grows in him,
And so his training began.
able to face any difficulty.
Years passed and Lkurus returned home,
But not all is peace and quiet.
New threats begin to fall
An army of demons comes to destroy. Lkurus and his family fled to the sanctuary,
Where wisdom and strength leave their mark,
With his sword, his shield and his skills,
Again in the fight he had to fight.
The enemies are stronger and better armed,
Lkurus faced a cruel enemy,
He fought tirelessly with all his might,
Until the army fell and disappeared into the setting sun. Victory again...
Although pain and loss are always present,
Lkurus showed his courage and bravery,
His people thank him for his bravery.
After the battle of Lkurus some time passed,
He reflected on everything that happened,
Thinking of his lost friends and family,
And he still feels this sadness deep inside.
But he knew he couldn't stop there,
'Cause there's always danger
His people need warriors like him,

Who can protect it with strength and skin. So he decided to
take the next step,
It will help other planets in danger,
Defend them with your wits and skills,
To play his part in the universe.
leave home and family.

He went into space in a spaceship,
Preparing for the next goku-style battle against namekusein,
And be prepared to face all the difficulties that come your way.
Thus Lkurus became a legendary warrior,
Travel the universe and fight against evil,
Hero engraved in rock forever in the annals of history,
As an example of outstanding courage and bravery.

The Warriors
1400 AD in the great Tenochtitlan
Aztec warriors were very brave,
Among them Dolinio, a warrior who feared for his might,
He is the best in battle arts.
But one day the sky darkened,
Strange creatures fell from above,
aliens have never seen this place,
Constant chaos and horror. The Aztecs had lost
and the emperor Moctezuma, looking for a solution,
Then his lightning was found on his sleeve,
The group of soldiers led by Dolinio has great strength and
remarkable achievements.
A group of warriors ready for battle,
With your weapons, cunning and courage,
They will not be defeated, they will defend their homeland,
With great honor they will preserve life in their kingdom. With
hearts full of courage themselves and the desire to protect their
homeland,
Dolinio and his Aztec warriors,
They are preparing for battle with great zeal.
Aliens are powerful, yes.
But they did not know the cunning of the Aztecs,
Then, with unmatched skill,
A group of warriors approached with majestic vigor. The fight
was fierce, without truce or rest,
Dolinio led the attack with great enthusiasm,
He shakes the earth and the air with his onyx mallet,
Hit the enemy mercilessly.
Victory seemed close, but they weren't sure

Because they knew that the aliens would not give up.
And with shia seeds, this is how the Aztec warriors regained their strength.
They were ready for the next battle very fiercely.
Dolino and his warriors,
They will face more difficulties,
But his courage and his strength do not falter,
Fight for your kingdom bravely and honestly.

Dolinio and his warriors, tired but victorious,
They returned to Tenochtitlan, praised for their great deeds,
But they know the fight isn't over
More danger lurks in the jungles of Mexico.
Moctezuma, the wise and cunning ruler,
He called the mighty before him,
And told them stories of the old gods,
and its possible extraterrestrial connection. Warriors who yearn for adventure and knowledge,
They decided to search in the jungle,
Searching for clues to the connection between gods and aliens,
This allows us to understand and combat unknown threats.
Guided by their cunning and great skill,
Dolinio and his warriors entered the jungle,
After walking for hours,
They arrived at an ancient temple full of mysteries and wonders.
In the temple they found ancient writings and relics,
Who spoke of the ancient gods and their power,
Strange creatures may also come,
Those who defy the gods with their arrogance and cruelty.

Warriors pay attention to signs and messages,
They decided to prepare for the final battle,
So they train harder and harder,
But just when they were training, some disturbing news came,
Even stranger creatures enter the jungle,
The final battle is coming
With Dolinio and his warriors as the last line of defense.

The day of battle has come.
Dolinio and his warriors are ready,
Raise your hand and courage
Defend your kingdom and your people.
Strange creatures have come to Tenochtitlan,
With their weapons and advanced technology,
ready to conquer the city
And they take what they want. The battle was fierce and bloody,
Warriors fell on both sides,
But Dolinio and his army of Aztec warriors,
They didn't give up for a second.
With his hand-to-hand combat skills,
and their old war tactics,
seek to weaken and confuse the enemy,
Give your allies time to attack. shells and drums,
With the shouts of soldiers,
The air is filled with the noise of war,
It made the ground shake underfoot.
Finally, using coordinated attacks,
Dolinio and his Aztec warriors,
successfully defeated the foreign invaders,

And return peace to Tenochtitlán. Moctezuma thanks the brave warriors,
and gives them the greatest honor,
For your courage, skill and sacrifice,
They saved their kingdom from destruction.
Dolinio and his Aztec warriors,
They became legends and role models.
For the next generation of Mexicans
They respect their history and traditions to the end. Thus the story of the Aztec warrior,
engraved in the collective memory,
As a symbol of courage and defiance,
Face unknown threats.

Until the end
In ancient times in a distant town,
Arkilo and his people live in peace and without worries. But one day the invaders arrived,
Thirst for blood and great treasures. Arkilo summoned his brave warriors,
Defend your home and your loved ones. With their sharp swords and their burning hearts,
They are ready for the toughest and fiercest battles. The attackers advance without mercy or fear,
But Arkilo's warriors did not succumb to pain. They fought bravely and never backed down,
Because when they win, they demand victory no matter the consequences. War day and night, without end,
But the warriors did not give up in the end. Arkilo led every fight and obstacle...
A firm faith that protected his life. The town turned into a sea of flames, the ground turned red,
But Arkilo's warriors were not alone. They fought with their last might to the end,
The invaders withdrew without recovering their wealth. Victory came, but at a high price,
Arkilo and his warriors paid for the attack with many lives. But their spirit and courage remain to this day in the graves under the sands,
They show that the alliance has the strength to win the war. Today, the story of these warriors continues,
In every soul that refuses to give in to despair. The town is in ruins, but the memory lives on,
The legacy of the warriors will always be one of adventure.

Thank you

2023

9 798223 939245